INDIANA JONES™

and the
KINGDOM OF
THE CRYSTAL SKULL™

W9-BKA-453

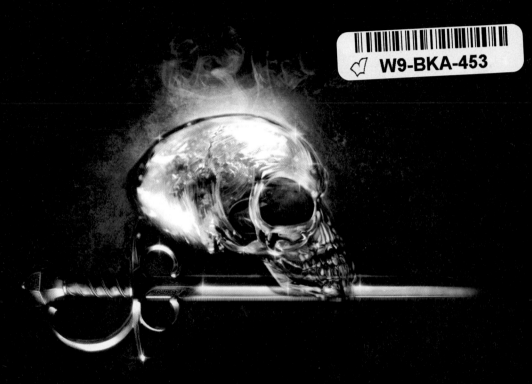

RACE FOR AKATOR

by Benjamin Harper

Based on the story by George Lucas and Jeff Nathanson
and the screenplay by David Koepp

LUCAS BOOKS

Scholastic Inc.

New York   Toronto   London   Auckland   Sydney
Mexico City   New Delhi   Hong Kong   Buenos Aires

No part of this publication may be reproduced in whole or in part, or stored
in a retrieval system, or transmitted in any form or by any means, electronic,
mechanical, photocopying, recording, or otherwise, without written permission
of the publisher. For information regarding permission, write to Scholastic Inc.,
Attention: Permissions Department, 557 Broadway, New York, NY 10012.

ISBN-13: 978-0-545-00702-3
ISBN-10: 0-545-00702-X

© 2008 by Lucasfilm Ltd. & ™. All rights reserved. Used under authorization.

Published by Scholastic Inc. SCHOLASTIC and associated logos are
trademarks and/or registered trademarks of Scholastic Inc.

Printed in the U.S.A.
First printing, September 2008

Russian spies were holding Mutt's mother, Marion, and Indy's friend, Ox, as prisoners. In order to free them, Indiana Jones and Mutt Williams needed to find a legendary crystal skull.

The mysterious skull was the key to locating an ancient city called Akator. The Russians needed Indy's help to find the lost city of gold.

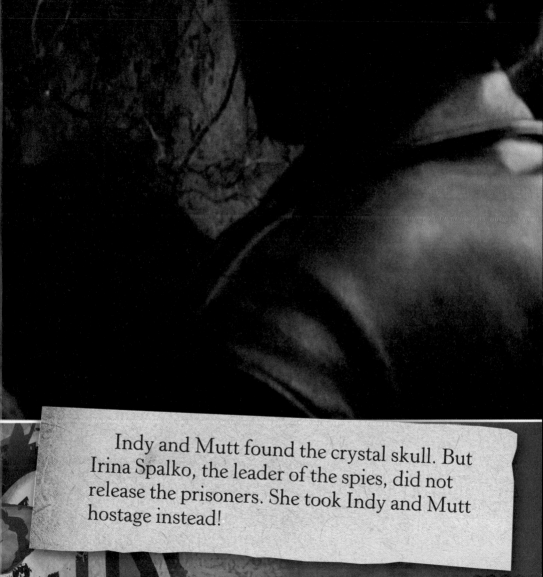

Indy and Mutt found the crystal skull. But Irina Spalko, the leader of the spies, did not release the prisoners. She took Indy and Mutt hostage instead!

Indy's friend Ox had once tried to find Akator.
Irina wanted Indy to tell her what Ox knew.
But it wouldn't be easy. Ever since Ox returned
from his adventure to Akator, he had been
acting oddly and saying strange things.

Professor Jones couldn't understand some of the things Ox was saying, such as, "Through eyes I last saw in tears." But parts of what Ox was saying *did* make sense. Indy showed Irina Spalko an area on a map where he thought they would find the city.

The Russians tied up Indy, Marion, and Mutt in the back of a truck. Ox was in another. They were driving through the jungle toward Akator. Indy needed to think fast, free himself and his friends, and take back the crystal skull!

Bam! Indy broke free and knocked out the guard.
He untied Marion and Mutt. Now he had to get Ox
and the skull away from the spies!

"Marion, take the wheel!" Indy called. She drove as Indy made his next move.

They caught up to the truck with Ox inside. Indy leaped over. But a Russian soldier grabbed the skull from Ox and threw it to Irina Spalko, who was in another car!

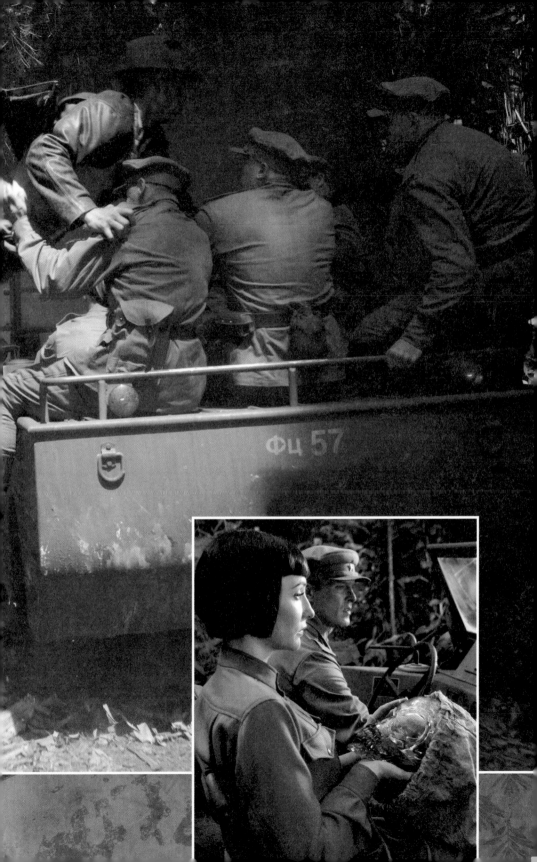

Irina Spalko had the skull, but Mutt had a plan to get it back. Marion raced the truck forward until they were even with Spalko's car. Then Mutt grabbed a sword he had found in the back of the truck and leaped across to attack.

Фц 57

Mutt and Irina jumped from one car to the other, fighting as they sped through the jungle. Mutt was battling as best he could, but Irina was better with the sword.

Indy raced to help. As Irina was pushing Mutt off the car they were fighting on, Indy zoomed in and *boom!* Mutt landed on the hood of Indy's truck.

Just then, Mutt turned around and was caught by a low-hanging tree branch!

As he watched the trucks roar away through the jungle, Mutt found himself stuck in a tree, surrounded by monkeys.

The monkeys darted away from Mutt, some swinging on vines. Mutt copied them and swung from a vine right into the passenger seat of Irina's car! Before she knew it, he had grabbed the crystal skull and had jumped onto the car's hood.

Mutt next jumped from Irina's car onto Indy's. The crystal skull was theirs once again!

Indy, Mutt, and Ox were safe for the moment.
Indy hit the gas and raced the Russians along a cliff.
Marion followed behind in her vehicle.

Indy rounded a corner in the trail. Up ahead was a huge dirt mound. He slammed on his brakes, but not fast enough—his truck went soaring through the air and slammed right into the side of the mound!

Everyone was scrambling out of their vehicles when Indy felt something bite him. They had landed on a giant anthill! All at once, thousands of ants ran out of the dirt, covering everything.

"Army ants!" Indy yelled. "Everyone out!"

They were all running from the ants when one of the soldiers tackled Indy. But Jones told Ox and Mutt to keep running away!

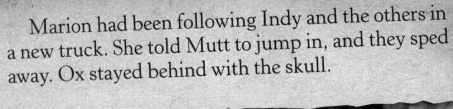

Marion had been following Indy and the others in a new truck. She told Mutt to jump in, and they sped away. Ox stayed behind with the skull.

But they didn't get far—the road dead-ended at a cliff! Marion looked over the edge and saw a river. She looked back at her truck, which was made to drive on land and in water. Marion had an idea!

Marion turned the truck around. Indy and Ox leaped into her vehicle and she drove back toward the cliff.

"You gotta stop this thing or we're going over the edge!" Indy yelled.

"That's the idea," Marion responded. And *whoosh!* over the cliff they went!

Down they plunged, into the river.

"Way to go, Mom!" Mutt called as they floated down the river away from the spies. But as they drifted downstream, the current started moving faster—they were headed straight toward a waterfall!

Before Indy and his friends knew it, they had splashed over the waterfall. And another fall was just ahead. But there was nothing they could do—they were swirling out of control down the winding jungle river.

They held on tight and splashed over the next waterfall. They were not out of danger yet!

They fell over yet another waterfall. The last one was the worst. Indy, Marion, Mutt, and Ox were all thrown from the truck and splashed into the rapids below, where they were dragged through the choppy waters of a roaring river.

Downriver, the water finally calmed. They were all okay! Ox sat on the shore with the crystal skull, which was making a strange humming sound. They looked around. In the mountain behind them, a giant head had been carved into the rock. Water was pouring out of the head's left eye.

"Through eyes I last saw in tears," Ox said. Indy looked at the waterfall—it all made sense to him now. He knew the way to Akator!

"We're going up there. The skull has to be returned," Indy said.

Ox led the way up the cliff face and through the head's left eye.

They passed through tunnels covered with ancient art, until they came to a chamber decorated with thirteen huge skeletons seated atop enormous thrones. They had made it to the legendary lost city of gold, Akator!